NUTCRACKER
and
SWAN LAKE

Given to: Innes
        Antoniades

from:
        Sara + mike
Summer '81
        England.

NUTCRACKER
and
SWAN LAKE

BY

WILLIAM APPLEBY

and

FREDERICK FOWLER

Illustrated by

AUDREY WALKER

LONDON

OXFORD UNIVERSITY PRESS

MELBOURNE   TORONTO

Oxford University Press, Walton Street, Oxford OX2 6DP

OXFORD LONDON GLASGOW NEW YORK
TORONTO MELBOURNE WELLINGTON
CAPE TOWN NAIROBI DAR ES SALAAM
TOKYO KUALA LUMPUR SINGAPORE JAKARTA HONG KONG
DELHI BOMBAY CALCUTTA MADRAS KARACHI

ISBN 0 19 314924 9

First Edition 1960
Seventh impression 1980

PRINTED IN GREAT BRITAIN

CONTENTS

NUTCRACKER

SWAN LAKE

All ready for the party

CHAPTER I

CHRISTMAS EVE

THIS is the story of a <u>nutcracker</u>—a very special nut-cracker, as you will see. It begins late in the afternoon on Christmas Eve, in a big room in a big house in Germany many years ago.

Clara and her brother Frank were going to give a party, and the room was all ready for the occasion. At one end there was a magnificent Christmas tree with a silver star at its tip. On the branches were coloured candles: red ones, yellow ones, green, blue, and white ones, all waiting to be lit. Other branches were bending under the weight of parcels in gay wrappings.

Beside the Christmas tree stood a huge table, almost touching the walls on either side. It was covered with a gleaming white cloth, and on the cloth were plates filled with sandwiches, pies, rich crumbly cake, shiny fruit, sweets, nuts, and all the other things you must have at Christmas.

Overhead were paper-chains and streamers, and in the middle of the room was a large open space for dancing and games.

Soon the room would be noisy and full of people. But now there was neither sound nor movement except for the quiet ticking of the clock on the wall. The chairs sat gazing at each other across the floor. The Christmas tree, torn from its friends in the forest, looked lonely. It was spending its first Christmas indoors and was wondering what was going to happen. Little did it know what surprising events it would see before the night was over!

★   ★   ★   ★

The door opened and Clara came into the drawing-room, ready for the party in a long, frilly dress. She was ten years old. She glanced at the tree, the table, and the chairs, to make sure that everything was all right; then she went to the window to watch for the first guests arriving.

What a marvellous sight met her eyes as she looked down into

the market square! Snow had
been falling for several hours,
and the dark sky told of still
more to come. The Town Hall
with its little towers was like
an iced Christmas cake made
for a giant; the church tower,
with white hat and clock face,
was like an overgrown snow-
man. People were hurrying
about doing last-minute

Christmas shopping, their heavy coats buttoned up to the top. Feet left deep patterns on the white carpet. Long ribbons of light from shop doorways and windows shone on the snow, making it sparkle. Some children were having a snowball fight, running backwards and forwards as they pelted each other, shouting with excitement.

Frank came into the room, dressed in his best velvet suit. He was two years older than Clara. His face looked freshly scrubbed and his hair was plastered down firmly. 'Anyone coming yet?' he asked. 'No, not yet,' replied Clara, who continued to stare out of the window. When Frank saw she was not looking he took two or three almonds from the table and put them into his mouth. He would have liked to try the sweets, but someone might notice a space if he took one. Instead he looked for his parcel on the tree and was pleased to find that it was nice and large.

At that moment Clara cried 'They're coming!' and he ran to join her at the window. The first guests were crossing the square, laughing and chatting as they came. 'Race you to the front door,' shouted Frank. Off he went, but Clara, unable to run in her long dress, followed him more slowly. When she reached the hall Frank had already opened the door to a group of excited children who were busily stamping their feet on the step to get rid of the snow. Soon overcoats, hats, gloves, and scarves were being removed and shoes changed. There was a constant knocking at the front door as more guests arrived. The girls lingered in front of the mirror, smoothing out their frills and curls. Then they joined the boys in the drawing-room, waiting for the party.

Some of the presents

CHAPTER II

CLARA'S PRESENT

Now the party was beginning. Old Hans, the musician, raised his fiddle to his chin, plucked the strings to see if they were in tune, and started to play. First they had musical chairs. Everyone, young and old, joined in except Granny. She was sitting in a straight-backed chair, determined not to miss a thing and thinking of the times when she had joined in the same game, many years ago. Next came a slow and stately dance for the grown-ups, while the children played follow-my-leader.

So the party went on, with lots of games and dances, until it was time to cut down the parcels from the tree. Frank and Clara quickly snipped the strings and handed out the presents to the excited children. There was a Jack-in-the-box, a trumpet, a woolly dog, and a toy gun. Clara herself got a beautiful doll with dark curly hair and eyes that opened and shut. Frank had a box of fierce-looking soldiers.

Next, refreshments were served. For the first time since the party began, silence fell on the room. Even the boys were quiet,

Uncle Dross arrives

for they could not make much noise with their mouths full of sandwiches and cake. This did not last long, however, for soon Uncle Dross, with red face and snow-white hair, came puffing in, saying, 'Sorry I'm late.' He always came late to these parties, for he could not come until he had served his last customer, put out the lights, and closed his shop for the Christmas holiday.

There was not another quiet moment until the party was over. As fast as one game ended Uncle Dross thought of another. The time flew as they played hunt the thimble, blind man's buff, and

charades. In between they danced. Soon, too soon, it was time
for the party to end. The children gathered round the tree to
sing for Granny. She loved to hear the young, sweet voices singing the story of the first Christmas. The last carol had scarcely
ended when Uncle Dross said, 'Goodness me—the presents! I'd
forgotten all about them!' He disappeared and returned very

Follow-my-leader

quickly with a bulging sack. There was a parcel for everyone in
the room. He rushed round handing them out. 'No time to
undo them now,' he cried; 'wait till you get home.' For already
parents were arriving to collect their children. One by one the
guests departed, and as the chill night air rushed in through the
open front door there were cries of 'Thank you for a wonderful
party', and 'A Merry Christmas to you all!'

When the last visitor had gone, Frank and Clara opened their presents from Uncle Dross. More toy soldiers for Frank, but this time he had also got a fort, complete with drawbridge, portcullis, battlements, and a cannon. 'Whatever have I got?' cried Clara. 'Why, they are nutcrackers!' But they were no ordinary ones, for the hard, dark wood of which they were made was carved in the form of a soldier. Every detail was there: the helmet above watchful eyes, the strong chin, the breastplate, the drawn sword. He seemed much more ready to crack skulls than nuts.

'Let me look!' said Frank, snatching the nutcrackers from Clara. 'Give them back to me!' shouted Clara, struggling with him. 'Now you two,' said their father; 'don't spoil Christmas by quarrelling. Give them back to her, Frank. It's time you were both in bed, anyway.'

Clara stroked the nutcrackers gently, to see that they had come to no harm. She put them down carefully on a chair whilst Frank arranged his fort and soldiers on the table. Then the two children went upstairs together quite happily.

Clara tiptoed downstairs

CHAPTER III

THE NUTCRACKER AND THE MOUSE KING

CLARA could not sleep. She tossed and turned on her little bed, but the excitement of the party had left her wide awake. She tried lying first on one side, then on the other, and then on her back. She tried a high pillow, a low one, and no pillow at all. She counted hundreds of sheep, but still sleep would not come to her. She wondered what time it was, but the blackness of the room only told her that it was still night. What a long night it was! Would Christmas Day never come? Thinking of Christmas reminded Clara of the stocking hanging at the foot of the bed. She got out carefully and groped her way towards it. There it was, still flat and empty. Getting back into bed and snuggling down under the bedclothes, she started thinking about her nutcrackers: 'Poor nutcracker soldier, lying downstairs all alone in a strange, dark room. I wish I had brought him to bed with me.' Suddenly she decided to fetch him. 'If I'm careful no one will hear me,' she thought, 'and it will only take a minute or two.' Again she tossed the bedclothes aside and got out of bed. In the darkness she groped for her slippers and felt her way to the door.

Opening it slowly, an inch at a time, for fear it squeaked, Clara tiptoed on to the landing. Like a blind man she moved along towards the staircase, one hand stretched before her pawing the air, the other stroking its way along the wall. Suddenly the wall ended and both her hands moved in space, like the feelers of a butterfly. She knew she had reached the stairs. She found the banisters and grasped them firmly, counting the steps under her slippered feet. Suddenly the church clock struck. Was it one o'clock? No—it boomed out again. Another boom, and another, and another. The last stroke died away and Clara had counted twelve. It was only midnight. She had left her bedroom on Christmas Eve, and now it was Christmas Day. When all was quiet she moved again and was soon at the drawing-room door. She opened it very quietly.

Clara's heart missed several beats. She stifled a scream. Her eyes almost popped out of her head, for brilliant moonlight lit the room, and the floor was alive with hundreds of mice! They were scampering into the room from all directions, popping up through holes in the skirting or darting in through the partly-open window. Some actually pattered over Clara's feet; she screamed and jumped on to a chair. The mice were on the look-out for food. Some of them had already discovered bits of broken biscuit lying about and were sitting nibbling furiously, with their tails stretched out behind them. Others had climbed up the Christmas tree and were chewing the remains of the coloured wax candles. Some were after the food and sweets on the table, trying to climb up its legs. But suddenly the toy

Battle!

soldiers sprang to life from fort and box and advanced on the invaders! Fierce fighting broke out on all sides. Here a gallant band of toy soldiers drove mice back into their hole with their swords. Over there a few brave soldiers, with backs to the wall and rifles raised, held a whole company of mice at bay. On the table, one soldier by brilliant sword-play forced a mouse to re-treat until, with a shriek, it plunged headlong over the edge.

Watching from her chair, Clara noticed one mouse much bigger and stronger than the others. He had long teeth, fierce-looking whiskers, and was wearing a purple cloak. He looked very important, and she felt sure he was the leader or even the

King of the Mice. He was in the middle of the floor fighting a duel with . . . Clara rubbed her eyes and looked again. Yes, it was! The King of the Mice was fighting a duel with her nutcracker soldier! Sparks flew as sword clashed upon sword. First one of them gave ground, then the other. Clara forgot everything else in the room as she watched her soldier fighting for his life. 'Go on, nutcracker, go on,'

The duel

she cried; 'beat him, beat him!' She gasped as her nutcracker slipped and fell to the ground. In an instant, the Mouse King had jumped on top of him and stood there laughing as he prepared to deliver the fatal blow. 'I *must* save him,' thought Clara. Taking off her slipper she threw it straight at the purple-cloaked figure; it hit him with a thwack between his beady eyes. At the same moment a dazzling light, like a great flash of lightning, hid everything from view.

All quiet again

CHAPTER IV

THE MAGIC JOURNEY

THE light blinded Clara for a while, but she knew that some great change had taken place in the room. There was no longer any noise of battle, clashing of swords, or shouts of victory. Everything was quite silent. Slowly, her eyes began to clear, and she looked about her. There was not a mouse in sight. Hundreds of them had been scampering and squealing in that very room only a few minutes before, and now they had all disappeared. Clara wondered if she had killed the Mouse King; if so, his followers must have carried his body away. The soldiers had not vanished like their enemies, but were all back where they came from, lying stiffly in their box or standing erect on the fort, just as if nothing had happened.

What of her nutcracker soldier? There was no sign of him;

but on the very spot where he had slipped and fallen, on the very spot where the Mouse King had jumped on him and raised his sword, stood a handsome Prince. He turned and came towards her. Taking her hand and bowing low he said, 'How can I repay you for saving my life?'

For a moment Clara was too surprised to say anything. Then she stammered, 'I-er-I was only trying to save my nutcracker soldier.' 'You *have* saved your nutcracker soldier,' replied the Prince, 'and you have also broken the spell which the King of the Mice had cast upon me. No longer am I a helpless wooden soldier, only used for cracking nuts. I am myself once more, a prince, free to come and go as I wish. And now I must be off with all speed to my own country. Would you like to come with me?' 'Your own country,' said Clara; 'what country is that?' 'I come from the Land of Sweets,' the Prince told her, 'and I must hurry home to the fairy Princess who has been waiting all this time for my return.' 'The Land of Sweets,' said Clara. 'I've never heard of it. I've seen packets and boxes and bottles of sweets, but I didn't know there was a land full of sweets. Is it a long way? How long will it take to get there?' 'Oh! it is thousands of miles away,' the Prince said, 'but I can take you there in half an hour or so. You will come, won't you?' It sounded so exciting that Clara almost said she would, but she thought of her parents and the dark, cold night outside, and the fact that it was Christmas Day. She could not be away from home at Christmas. The Prince must have known what she was thinking, for he suddenly said, 'No one will miss you. You will be back before dawn. Please, do come.' 'If I'm back before Father and Mother wake up, I'll be delighted to come,' Clara replied.

'Splendid!' said the Prince and threw his cloak around her. She had a strange feeling: what was happening to her? Her feet were leaving the ground and her head was up amongst the streamers! Now she was floating through the air and out of the room hand

Dancing with the snowflake fairies

in hand with the Prince! She saw her home and the market square getting smaller and smaller. Soon they reached the forest on the mountain side and were gliding between its snow-covered trees. Overhead, the moon looked down on them and the wind sighed softly through the branches. Clara did not feel cold, although by this time she was floating towards the mountain tops and a snowstorm was approaching. Neither did she feel lonely and afraid, for the Prince was by her side, leading her onwards.

Soon everything was blotted out by the whirling snow and then Clara had another surprise. As the snowflakes approached she saw that they were not made of real snow that sticks to clothes and makes eyes blink and cheeks tingle. Instead, each flake was a tiny white-clothed fairy, twirling and dancing in the sky. When a very large flake glided towards them Clara knew by the crown and the dazzling white dress that it was the Snow Queen. The Prince bowed and Clara tried to curtsey, but she found it difficult with her feet in the air. The Snow Queen smiled, took the Prince by the hand and waltzed away with him, whilst Clara and thousands of snowflake fairies danced round them in attendance. In between the mountain peaks they glided, down the valleys on the other side, and over the roofs of houses in strange villages. The dance continued as on and on they went until mountains were far behind and they could hear the waves of the sea breaking on a sandy shore. Above the beach, the Snow Queen and her attendants waved goodbye and turned to dance their way back to their home in the mountains.

Clara and the Prince floated gently down into a boat which appeared from nowhere. They were alone, but no sooner were they seated than the golden sail filled with a gentle breeze and the boat sped over the waves. The night was full of surprises for Clara; the sea through which they were speeding was one of them. She had never seen the sea before, but she had heard her mother and father talking about it and she had read about it in books. This sea was not at all what she had expected—cold bluey-green, with huge foam-tipped waves tossing boats about like corks. Instead, it was a beautiful rose-pink in colour, and its tiny waves were tinged with silver. It did not look cold at all and it was calm and flat like a pond. Clara was so fascinated that she forgot the Prince was by her side and she was startled when his voice suddenly broke the stillness.

'Can you see anything on the horizon?' he asked. 'Look straight in front of you.' Clara looked, and away in the distance

Clara reaches the Land of Sweets

she could see a small speck which grew larger every minute. 'It's too big for a boat,' she exclaimed, after looking at it for a while; 'is it an island?' 'It is indeed,' replied the Prince; 'it is the Land of Sweets. How thrilling it is to see my home again after all this time,' he went on, 'and my Sugar Plum Fairy too.' Clara was almost too excited to listen, for by this time they were quite near the island and she could see the beach, which she later found was made of brown sugar, and beyond it, rows and rows of brightly-coloured houses made of sweets. As the boat approached the shore, she saw people everywhere coming out of their houses and running over the sands to watch them arrive. She expected a terrible crash when the swiftly-moving vessel hit the shore, but instead, a huge wave lifted them in the air, and gently lowered the boat high and dry on the sugar sands.

'Welcome to my country,' said the Prince, as he helped Clara to disembark. She stepped out and felt land under her feet for the first time since leaving home. When she turned to look at the waiting crowd she stepped backward in surprise, for they were not people, but fairies; not the tiny fairies that hide in flowers or live under mushrooms, but real grown-up fairies as big as herself!

Clara meets Sugar Plum Fairy

CHAPTER V

THE LAND OF SWEETS

SUDDENLY there was a commotion at the back of the crowd, as fairy soldiers pushed their way through, crying, 'Make way, please, everybody, make way for Sugar Plum Fairy!' 'My Sugar Plum Fairy!' cried the excited Prince as he ran to meet her.

'Allow me to introduce Clara,' he said to her. 'This is the dear girl who saved my life.' Clara made a deep curtsey, a much more successful one this time. The Prince was telling Sugar Plum Fairy all about the battle, and the important part Clara had played. He said so many nice things about her that she felt herself blushing until she was sure her face was the same colour as Sugar Plum Fairy's dress. Clara had never seen such a magnificent dress. Its rich colour reminded her of the roses which bloomed every summer in the garden at home. It looked so light and fairy-like that Clara was sure its thread was the work of spinning spiders. Here and there it was studded with diamonds. More diamonds flashed round the Fairy's neck and still more twinkled in her hair. 'Welcome to our land,' she said to Clara. 'I, and all who live here, rejoice in the Prince's return, and we are deeply grateful to you for freeing him from the spell. Let me lead you to the palace; you must be our guest of honour at the celebrations.'

With fairy soldiers making a way for them through the delighted onlookers, Clara, the Prince, and Sugar Plum Fairy walked over the sands towards the gleaming white palace. Clara was not at all surprised to discover that it was made of white icing. She was no longer surprised by anything, for she had seen so many strange things since leaving her bedroom. She *would* have been if it had been made of ordinary stone or brick, like the buildings at home. The outside was decorated with piping and rosettes, just like the Christmas cake she had cut at her party. Silver pellets were embedded in the large doors of icing.

Once inside, Clara was led into a big ballroom which was even more magnificent. Its lofty roof was supported by twirling pillars of barley sugar. The walls were covered with hard, shining butterscotch. She walked across a floor of red and white tiles of Turkish Delight to a throne of marshmallow, where she was to sit and watch the performance. Round the sides of the room stood all the important people in the land, waiting for their guest to sit down before they themselves could be seated.

Very soon the entertainment began. There was a Spanish dance and an Arab dance, a Chinese dance and a Russian dance.

Clara enjoyed every one of them. She admired the Spanish costumes with their rich red silks and black velvet. She laughed until she almost cried at the funny, shuffling Chinamen, with their pigtails bobbing up and down behind them. The Russian dance, which got faster and faster and suddenly stopped, excited

The dance of the Sugar Plum Fairy

her. She loved the tiny little fairies who entered carrying toy flutes, which they played as they danced around, but better than everything else she liked the dance of the Sugar Plum Fairy. There was great applause when it was Sugar Plum Fairy's turn. Every eye in the room was fixed on her as she rose from her throne, walked to the centre of the floor, and performed a dainty and most fairy-like dance to a tinkly tune played by the orchestra. When it was over, she invited all the onlookers to join in the next dance, which was also the last one: the Waltz of the Flowers.

Clara danced with the Prince. As they waltzed, flower petals dropped through holes in the ceiling, twirling round the dancers

The petals fell like a snowstorm

before falling to the floor. At first Clara enjoyed watching them as she danced in the Prince's arms, but soon she began to feel afraid. Far too many petals were falling. If they did not stop soon everyone would be buried in them. Faster and faster they fell, until it was like a blinding snowstorm—white petals, pink petals, yellow petals, and blue petals—and the air was heavy with the scent of roses, lilies, sweet-peas, and carnations. Soon the feet of the dancers were buried in the flower-covered floor, and still the petals came down, until dancing was difficult and the music was muffled. After one very heavy shower of flowers Clara was completely covered. She lost the Prince, she could not see, and she could scarcely breathe as she struggled to free herself. 'Help! Help!' she shouted. As she opened her mouth, petals poured in. The more she struggled, the more she sank into the scented sea of flowers. She made one last great effort, with arms flying and legs kicking like a sinking swimmer. Petals flew in all directions as her head rose above them and her eyes blinked in the light.

Clara looked around her to see what had happened to the Prince and Sugar Plum Fairy, and could not believe her eyes. No Prince, no Sugar Plum Fairy, no Russians, Arabs, or Chinamen, no flower-petals, and not even the ballroom were to be seen. She was back home in bed, with the bed-clothes kicked on to the floor and the first light of Christmas Day coming in at the window. She could not believe it. She pinched herself to see if she was awake, but it was true enough. It was her own bed in her own room, and through the window she could see the familiar chimney-pots of her own town. Her stocking was still hanging at the foot of the bed, no longer lean and limp, but broad and bulging.

Home again

CHAPTER VI

CHRISTMAS MORNING

CLARA was too surprised to do anything but lie on the bed and think over the events of the night. Only a few minutes earlier she had been dancing with the Prince. All around her were other dancers. Where had they gone? Where was Sugar Plum Fairy? Where was the Prince? Were they all playing a joke on her? She expected that any minute her bedroom door would burst open and they would all rush in laughing.

Now someone was coming to the door and she sat up, but she quickly lay down again when she saw it was her mother. 'Merry Christmas,' said her mother gaily. 'Merry Christmas,' moaned Clara. 'Why! whatever is the matter?' her mother asked. 'Are you ill? You haven't even bothered to look in your stocking!'

* 24 *

'I've lost all my friends,' cried Clara; 'they've all left me!' 'Lost all your friends?' echoed her mother in amazement. 'Yes,' cried Clara 'I've lost the Prince, Sugar Plum Fairy, and all the people in the Land of Sweets.' 'Whatever are you talking about?' her mother asked. 'I was in the Land of Sweets a few minutes ago,' sobbed Clara, 'but I don't know what has happened to it.' 'Oh! I see,' said mother, 'you've been dreaming! Well, hurry up and get dressed; breakfast is nearly ready.'

When her mother had left the room Clara began slowly putting on her clothes. Had she been dreaming? She was sure it was not a dream. She was certain she had flown over the mountains with the Prince. She knew she had really seen the rose-pink sea, the brown-sugar sand, and the white-icing palace, and suddenly she knew how she could prove it. She quickly finished dressing and dashed straight down to the drawing-room. She looked all round it. She looked at the Christmas tree, the chairs, and the table. 'There,' she said to herself, 'I knew it wasn't a dream. The nutcrackers have gone!'

If she had only been dreaming, they would still have been lying on the chair in the drawing-room where she had left them the night before. They were not on the chair. They had not fallen under it. She searched everywhere, but the nutcrackers had disappeared. Clara knew why. She had actually seen them change into a prince. She alone had broken the spell.

CHAPTER VII

THE MUSIC

ALTHOUGH you had never perhaps heard of Clara and Prince Nutcracker before you started to read this book, it is not a new story. It is much older than you, or your father, or your grandfather. For more than a hundred years girls and boys, and grown-ups too, have read about Clara or had the story told to them. Most probably girls and boys in Germany heard it first, because it was first written down by a German story-teller named Hoffmann. He called it 'The Nutcracker and the King of the Mice'. Gradually this tale spread to other countries. It did not always have the same ending. Sometimes it ended by Clara staying in the Land of Sweets, and living there happily ever after with the Prince and Sugar Plum Fairy.

When our Nutcracker story reached Russia something very important happened to it, which helped to make it famous all over the world. Some Russians read it and decided to use it for a ballet. You most probably know of many stories which have been made into plays. Perhaps you have seen stories of Robin Hood played on television, or a famous story such as *Peter Pan* made into a play and performed at a theatre. The ballet is also a way of acting a story, but quite different from a play. In ballet there is no speaking. The performers tell the story by miming and dancing to the music of an orchestra. Because of all the dancing, music is always an important part of ballet.

Having decided to make the Nutcracker story into a ballet there was a lot to be done. Someone had to work out all the dance movements, someone had to write the music, and someone else had to design the costumes and scenery. Others were busy choosing the dancers and teaching them their steps. The person

A celesta

who wrote the music was the famous Russian composer Tchaikovsky. He had already written the music for two other famous ballets, *Swan Lake* and *The Sleeping Beauty*. Soon after he started to compose the music he had to leave his work, for he had to visit America. On his way there, he called in Paris, where he saw a new musical instrument, a celesta. He was delighted with it and decided to use one in the *Nutcracker* music. He had one sent to Russia to await his return from America. When he arrived home again he settled down to finish the music. The dancers were busy practising, the costumes and scenery were being made, and Tchaikovsky himself often played the piano at rehearsals. Finally, everything was ready and the *Nutcracker* had its first performance. The Tsar (King) of Russia was present, all the important people were at the theatre, and everyone was charmed by the music Tchaikovsky had written.

Today his *Nutcracker* music is known and enjoyed in most countries of the world. You may not be able to see a performance of the ballet, but you can still hear and enjoy the music. It is often played by orchestras at concerts and on the wireless and television, and you can also hear it on gramophone records. Do not be surprised if the records are labelled 'Casse Noisette Suite', because 'Casse Noisette' is French for 'Nutcracker' and the word Suite means a collection of pieces. The Dance of the Sugar Plum Fairy, the Russian Dance, the Chinese Dance, the Waltz of the Flowers, and other dances are all collected together in the 'Casse Noisette' Suite. Perhaps the first time you hear the music you may wonder which piece is which. Here are some clues. Tchaikovsky used the celesta he bought in Paris in 'The Dance of the Sugar Plum Fairy', so you will easily recognize this piece by its 'tinkly', bell-like melody, which sounds just like fairy music. Do you know what a glockenspiel is? You have probably seen one, even if you did not know its name, for toy glockenspiels are very popular and can be seen in most toy-shops. A glockenspiel is a row of flat metal bars of different lengths which make 'tinkly' sounds when struck by a small wooden hammer. A celesta is really a grown-up glockenspiel. It looks like a small piano. It has a keyboard, but if you look inside, you will find that the hammers strike flat metal bars instead of hitting strings.

You should not have any difficulty in recognizing the 'Russian Dance', or 'Trepak' as it is called. That was the dance which Clara found so exciting. It gradually gets faster and faster and then suddenly stops. The 'Chinese Dance' is quite different. From beginning to end it goes, 'pom-pom, pom-pom, pom-pom, pom-pom' on the bassoons, reminding you of a Chinaman waddling about. In it, you will hear the flutes too, and you will hear them again in the 'Dance of the Mirlitons', which means Dance of the Toy Flutes. You will recognize the 'Waltz of the Flowers' by the harp solo which comes at the beginning, and you are sure to know the March when you hear it, with its lively, 'left-right, left-right', just like a marching army. It will be a great help if you can play some of these lovely tunes yourself, so a few of them are arranged very simply at the end of this chapter. Try them on the piano, the violin, or your recorder.

When Christmas comes once more, remember Clara's exciting Christmas Eve of long ago. If you can, go and see the *Nutcracker* Ballet at the theatre. If you cannot go to a real live performance, look out for it on television. If you cannot see it at all, bring out the gramophone records and—a very enjoyable musical Christmas to you, when it comes!

THE DANCE OF THE SUGAR PLUM FAIRY
The tune on the celesta starts like this

TREPAK—RUSSIAN DANCE—the lively tune is first heard on the strings

CHINESE DANCE

Listen for the bassoon playing 'pom-pom' all the way through—
146 'pom-poms'!

pom-pom pom-pom

DANCE OF THE MIRLITONS (Toy Flutes)

Flutes

Some of the tunes from WALTZ OF THE FLOWERS

Horns

Flutes & Oboes

Violas & Cellos

Coming to the birthday party

CHAPTER I

PRINCE SIEGFRIED COMES OF AGE

THE great gardens of the castle were crowded with people. So was the road that climbed the hillside to the castle gateway. Every man, woman, and child in the country was coming that way, for the Queen's only son, Prince Siegfried, was twenty-one and this was his birthday party. Big as the castle was, it was not big enough to hold the thousands of guests, and so the party was taking place in the open air. The lawns and paths had become a huge fairground on which a bright sun shone from a cloudless sky. Some of the guests who had arrived early just stood and stared at the castle with its great round towers and battlements, its big gateway, and tiny slit-like windows. They had never been invited to a castle before! Others sat on the grass watching the country dances and listening to the music of the bands. The children dashed from the Punch and Judy Show to the performing bears, from the bears to the clowns, and then back to the Punch and Judy Show again. They also crowded round the large tables which had been set up in the shadow of the trees, loaded with food and drink. Some of them were already lost in the crowds, and anxious mothers ran hither and thither looking for them and calling their names.

Suddenly loud cheering was heard from the direction of the castle: Prince Siegfried was coming out to join his guests. Everyone ran to greet him. The Punch and Judy Show was left without an audience and even the food-tables were deserted. The Prince was dressed in costly silks and velvets, with a long cloak of red and gold, and looked very happy as he laughed and joked with his friends. He stopped here and there to greet some-one he knew, and bowed low when young girls curtseyed and offered him garlands. From all sides there were cries of 'Long live the Prince', and 'A Happy Birthday, Prince Siegfried'.

After visiting every corner of the gardens so that he could see all his guests, the Prince and his companions joined in the fun of the party. They danced with the girls from the villages until they were tired; then they sat down and watched the side-shows, laughing loudly at the clowns and applauding the conjurer.

Now the Queen arrived, and everybody cheered again. As she walked through the grounds followed by her Ladies-in-Waiting, there were gasps of admiration at her snow-white silken gown and her sparkling diamonds. The countrymen doffed their hats

Greeting Prince Siegfried

and bowed at her approach, whilst their wives curtseyed. After the Queen had passed by, the games and the dancing, the eating and the drinking started again and went on until dusk. As darkness fell, giant fireworks lit up the sky. Swishing rockets rose swiftly into the air and burst into many-coloured stars. Small children ran to hide behind their mothers, but soon peeped out again to watch the whirling pinwheels. The party ended when the Queen and the Prince appeared on one of the balconies and waved goodbye to their guests. Three mighty cheers rang out, scaring the sleeping birds in the trees and sending them fluttering away into the darkness. Gradually the countryfolk turned towards the gateway and began their homeward journeys, tired but happy. As they went along holding sleeping children in their arms they all said the same thing to each other: 'What a wonderful day we've had!'

Prince Siegfried alone in the garden

CHAPTER II

THE QUEEN'S WISH

I T was the following evening. Throughout the day workmen had been busy removing sideshows, tables, chairs, and every other trace of the party. Now they had finished their task: all was once more quiet and peaceful. Prince Siegfried walked alone up and down the garden paths, past the water-lily pools full of darting goldfish, and the beds of sweet-scented roses. He was no longer happy. He trod the paths with lowered head and hands clasped behind his back. He had no eyes for the beauty of the garden. He did not even look up when his dearest friend Benno came up to him.

Benno stood for a while waiting for the Prince to greet him, but Siegfried continued to walk in silence. At last Benno approached him, bowing low as he did so.

'Forgive me, dear Siegfried,' he said, 'but I am sorry to see you so unhappy. Are you unwell, or have you had bad news?'

The Prince looked up. 'Bad news indeed, dear Benno,' he replied. 'My mother, the Queen, has spoken to me today. I am afraid she does not like you, Benno, or any of my friends.'

'Oh dear!' exclaimed Benno, 'what have I done—what have we all done to offend her Majesty?'

'The Queen thinks that my friends encourage me to lead a lazy life of pleasure, and waste my time in dancing and sport,' answered the Prince. 'Now that I have come of age, Her Majesty insists that I must turn to more serious occupations and so prepare myself for the day when I am King.'

'Oh dear! Oh dear!' sighed Benno. 'When I think of the happy times we have had, the long days in the hunting-field, the merry nights of dancing and singing in the village inns, the——'

'Wait,' interrupted the Prince, 'I have not finished yet. I have not told you all. There is much worse to follow.'

'What could be worse than that?' Benno cried.

'I am to marry,' replied the Prince quickly.

'Marry?' said Benno; 'well, there's nothing wrong with that, but who on earth are you going to marry?'

'I don't know,' was the reply.

Benno was amazed. He stood there with his mouth open. At last he said, 'Do you mean that you are to marry someone you have never seen; someone you have never spoken to; someone you do not know?'

'That is so,' replied the Prince. 'My mother has invited six princesses to the Royal Ball tomorrow night. She insists that I must choose one of them as a bride. I have pleaded with her. I have told her that I do not wish to marry until I meet someone I love, but she will not listen to me. I cannot refuse her wishes. If the Queen commands, I must obey.'

They walked together in silence for a while, shocked by the Queen's order.

The swans

Suddenly there was a noise overhead. With slowly-flapping wings and long necks outstretched, more than a score of swans and cygnets were moving gracefully through the sky. Benno's sadness left him immediately.

'Come,' he cried, 'let's hunt the swans and forget our troubles for a bit.' The Prince showed no enthusiasm, so Benno pleaded with him. 'Please come, dear Siegfried. It may be our last chance of hunting together.'

'Very well,' agreed the Prince, and together they quickly made their way to the castle to get horses and crossbows and summon their friends. Soon they were all galloping across fields and over hedges and ditches. A cry from one of the party announced that the swans had been sighted, circling above a nearby forest. Round they flew, dropping lower and lower each time, until they were lost in the trees. The forest with its darkness and tangled undergrowth was no place for horses, so the riders dismounted and continued the chase on foot. There was a lake deep in the heart of the forest and there they hoped that they would find the swans.

By the lake

CHAPTER III

A MEETING AT MIDNIGHT

NIGHT was falling as the hunters entered the forest, and in the darkness Siegfried soon lost touch with his companions. So he made his own way to the lake. When he got to it he sat down on a log to rest and wait.

'What a beautiful night' he thought, looking round him. The smooth surface of the water shone like silver in the moonlight. The warm air was still and the trees were silent. Across the lake he could see a ruined chapel, perched on the edge of tall cliffs.

He had almost forgotten about the swans when suddenly he

saw them flying low and coming in his direction. He quickly hid
behind a tree, tightening his hands on his bow. As the birds flew
nearer, Siegfried saw that one, more beautiful than the others,
flew as if it was the leader. The swans flew so low that their
breasts skimmed the lake's surface, and then rose again from the
water. Siegfried realized that they would land on the grassy shore
in front of him, and prepared to shoot as they landed. Suddenly
he became numb with amazement, so that the bow fell from his
hands. As each bird touched the grass it changed into a beautiful
maiden clothed from head to foot in a long white dress! The
cygnets became lovely children, and all gathered round the
leader, who was dressed like the others, but wore a crown. From
a distant church tower came the chimes of midnight.

The Prince ran towards them. When they saw him they
were afraid and tried to reach the cover of the trees. 'Stop,'
he cried; 'I will not harm you!' The leader turned and faced
him.

'You have a bow there on the ground,' she said. 'You are a
hunter and mean to kill us.'

'No, no,' said Siegfried, 'I promise not to harm you. But I
don't understand. A minute ago you were swans flying over a
lake, and now you are beautiful maidens who speak my language.
My name is Siegfried. Pray tell who you are.'

'I am called Odette,' said the leader of the swans, coming
nearer, 'and our story is a sad one. Many years ago I was a
princess living in a palace far away. One day I was carried off by
an evil magician who took me to his castle and changed me into
a swan. My friends here were also taken from their homes and
turned into swans. Our parents weep, for they think we are dead.

They searched the world, but never found us. As the hour of midnight strikes we become ourselves again, but only for a short time. When day breaks and the first rays of light touch us we become swans again, forced by our wicked master's spell to fly back to him.'

'This is an outrage,' cried the Prince. 'Who is this evil person? Tell me his name and where he lives, for he must die!'

'It is good of you to wish to help us,' Odette answered, 'but I am afraid it is no use. The magician's name is Rothbart, but you will not catch him, for he is a master of disguise. That tree over there may be Rothbart, or that small cloud up there, watching us and hearing every word. Perhaps he has changed into an animal, or a toadstool, and is quite near us now, hiding in the grass.'

'Does that mean that you and your friends must always be swans?' asked Siegfried. 'Can nothing be done to help you?'

'I must remain a swan until I meet someone who loves me— someone who loves me so much that he would willingly die for me. Then the spell will be broken and I and all my companions will be free again. But what chance have I of meeting anyone when I am a swan all day and only a human being when everyone else is asleep?'

At that moment Benno and the rest of the party came up. The maidens were frightened by the crossbows they carried, but Siegfried quickly put everyone at ease. He told his friends what had happened, introduced them to Odette and her friends, and very soon they were all talking and laughing together as if they had known each other for years. When they were tired of talking they danced together on the springy green turf. The men

They all talked and danced together

were determined to stay until dawn and prevent the maidens changing to swans again. After dancing they rested while the cygnets danced for them, and Odette did a solo dance. 'How beautiful she is!' thought the Prince as he watched her; 'I have never seen anyone so lovely.' Finally, as dawn approached, they all danced together again.

'Odette,' whispered the Prince as he held her in his arms, 'if you must soon become a swan again and leave me, please promise that you will return here again tomorrow night.'

'I will try,' she replied, 'but if Rothbart suspects anything he will do all in his power to prevent me.'

Suddenly the Prince remembered the Royal Ball.

'Oh no,' he cried, 'I had almost forgotten: I can't meet you here tomorrow night, after all.' He went on to tell Odette all about the ball.

'And so, you see,' he ended, 'my mother is forcing me to choose a bride tomorrow night. Odette, Odette! Please come to the ball yourself,' he pleaded. 'Then I can choose you to be my bride, for I have loved you since the first moment I saw you. I promise to love you and you alone as long as I live. Please say you will come.'

There was silence for a while and then Odette whispered, 'I love you too, Siegfried, but I am afraid. If Rothbart is listening he will do us evil.'

So absorbed were they in each other that they did not see the faint silver streaks growing in the night sky.

'You will promise to come——' Siegfried never finished his sentence, for at that moment the maidens became swans again and flew from the arms of their partners. The men stood, powerless to do anything, as the birds flew out over the lake, gained height, and

Odette and Siegfried

disappeared over the tree-tops. A sad and disappointed Siegfried led his party homeward. The lakeside was deserted again, save for a solitary owl which blinked down from a branch. It was a real owl and yet it was not, for it was Roth-bart in disguise. He had seen and heard everything and there was a wicked gleam in his eyes.

With wings slowly flapping, he flew from the branch and followed the swans.

The ball begins

CHAPTER IV

AT THE BALL

THE Ballroom was ablaze with colour. Guests from many
lands were present in their national costumes. Many of
the men wore the gold-braided red or blue uniforms of
their regiments. Massed flowers in full bloom hid the walls from
view and clothed the marble pillars. Hundreds of candles were
twinkling up above.

Suddenly a fanfare rang out, the tall golden doors at one end
of the castle ballroom opened, and the royal procession entered.
It moved slowly through the throng of guests, towards the two
thrones which stood on a small platform at the far end of the
room.

When the Queen and Prince Siegfried were seated, the band

up above in the minstrel's gallery played the opening bars of a waltz, the guests took partners, and the Royal Ball had begun.

On another night Siegfried would have enjoyed every minute of the evening, as he was an excellent dancer. But this time he was in no mood for pleasure. Dance followed dance, but he just sat there gazing into space. Even the foreign dancers from Spain and Hungary, Poland and Russia left him unmoved. As each dance ended there was cheering and clapping and cries of 'Encore', but Siegfried still sat like one in a dream.

At last the dreaded moment arrived. The trumpets rang out and the six princesses entered. They curtseyed to the Queen and to the Prince, and then retired some distance away. Siegfried's ordeal was about to begin. He had to meet each princess in turn and dance with her. He had no desire to dance with any of them, but, not wishing to be rude, he took the hand of each girl, as she was introduced, danced without showing any enthusiasm and scarcely said a word. Which one should he choose? This one? That one? He was still determined not to choose any one of them. As he sat down again the Queen turned towards him. 'Tell us, dear Siegfried, which of the princesses will you marry?' All eyes were turned in his direction. There was silence in the room as Siegfried hesitated in his reply, for he knew his answer would deeply offend the Queen.

Fortunately for him the trumpets rang out suddenly as two unexpected guests arrived: a knight, clad from head to foot in black armour, leading a girl towards the thrones. For the first time during the evening Siegfried sat up straight with excitement. Was it Odette who had just come in with this strange black knight? She looked like the girl whom he had seen the

He rose to meet her

night before in the forest, the
girl who had changed into a
swan and flown away—and yet
there was something different
about her. The newcomers
came nearer and the Prince
gripped the arms of his throne.
Yes, it was Odette; he was
sure it was the girl he had invited to the ball. There was
certainly something strange
about her, but that was most
probably because she was
dressed differently. By the
side of the lake she had worn
a long white gown and he had
seen her only in the moon-

light. Now her dress was of black and the jewels round her neck sparkled as they caught the light from many candles. 'Welcome, Odette,' said the Prince as he rose to meet her. Silently she took his hand, the band started to play, and they danced together. 'Odette,' he whispered as they glided round the room, 'I thought you were never coming.' She looked up at him and smiled.

A swan beating its wings against the windows

He was so happy that he did not see a swan beating its wings against one of the windows.

As the dance ended Siegfried took his partner's hand and led her towards his mother. 'Your Majesty,' he said, 'I have chosen my bride. I wish to marry this girl.' The Queen nodded her approval and many of the guests came up to offer their congratulations.

Still no one noticed the swan outside beating its wings against one of the windows.

The knight in black armour stepped forward, bowing first to the Queen and then to the Prince. 'May it please Your Majesty,' he said, 'this is my daughter. I consent to her marrying your son, if he will swear to love her and no other woman until he dies.' The Prince laughed aloud and said, 'That is a request I grant gladly. I swear I will love your daughter and no other as long as I live.' Turning to the girl, the Prince solemnly repeated his oath. 'I love you with all my heart, and I swear always to be faithful to you.'

As he said these words there was a blinding flash and the Black Knight and his daughter vanished. A terrific thunderstorm burst over the castle. The ballroom rocked under the violent peals of thunder and vivid lightning lit the room. At last Siegfried saw the swan beating its wings against the window. It was Odette. Immediately he realized he had been tricked. The Black Knight was Rothbart. The girl was Rothbart's daughter, and he had just promised to love her until he died. Stricken with grief he dashed out into the night to find Odette.

The swans return

THE RESCUE

ODETTE, still in the form of a swan, turned away from the castle windows just as Siegfried set out to search for her. Wearily she flew to rejoin her companions. Her wings were battered and bruised and she was desperately unhappy. She had done her best to warn the Prince, but alas he had not seen her until it was too late. With difficulty she continued her flight, for her wings were becoming more painful. She wished that she were dead.

Her friends were slowly circling above the lake when at last she arrived. Odette flew with them until twelve strokes rang out from the church tower, and they became human again as they touched the shore. Immediately they crowded round her, anxious to know what had happened, but before she uttered a word they knew from her sad expression and her tears that they had not yet escaped from Rothbart's power. At last, in a voice scarcely louder than a whisper, Odette told them what she had seen. When they heard of Rothbart's cunning, her friends tried to comfort her, though in their hearts they were as sad and disappointed as she was. Their hope of freedom had been dashed. Odette came to the end of her story. 'Rothbart has triumphed again,' she said, 'and we are doomed to be swans for the rest of our lives.' There was a long silence, for they were all too disheartened to speak or move. They neither saw nor heard someone approaching. It was the Prince. He had come as fast as he could in search of Odette, but when he saw her his steps faltered, for he did not know how she would receive him.

'Oh, Odette,' he cried, when at last he took her in his arms, 'please forgive me.' There was another silence and then Odette whispered, 'There is nothing to forgive, dear Siegfried. I told you how powerful and evil Rothbart is. I have been in his power so long that I fear I shall never escape.'

The storm, which had ceased for a while, now broke out again more violently than before. Heavy rainfall made them all run to the trees for shelter. As they crouched together under the dripping branches, the cold and damp added to their unhappiness.

'Surely there is some way out of our troubles,' Siegfried kept saying.

'No,' was Odette's reply, 'I am doomed to remain a swan. Rothbart will never let me go. There is only one thing to be done——'

'What is it?' said Siegfried eagerly.

Rothbart!

'You must leave me,' was the reply. 'Leave me and forget me, for I shall never be free to marry you.'

'Forget you?' cried the Prince, 'that I will never . . .'

His reply was interrupted by a piercing cry from Odette. She was pointing upwards as she cried out, and Siegfried saw with horror, sitting above them in the branches, an enormous owl. Its cruel eyes stared down at them; its pointed beak seemed twisted into an evil grin. Rothbart, in his owl-like disguise, had come to gloat over them!

Siegfried felt for some weapon. If only he could kill this evil bird perhaps all their troubles would disappear. But he was unarmed. He had hurried from the ballroom carrying neither sword nor crossbow. He turned to Odette—but she was no longer by his side!

'Odette,' he cried, 'where are you?' He tried to see through the gloomy trees, running anxiously this way and that, crying 'Odette, Odette!' At last a vivid flash of lightning turned night into day for a moment, and he saw her running towards the lake.

'Come back, come back,' he shouted as he raced after her.

When she reached the water Odette turned and ran along the shore towards a steep cliff. She realized that she was being followed, quickly scrambled up to the top of its rocky slopes, and stood swaying near the edge. Below her she could see the angry waves breaking into foam.

'Odette, come back!' the Prince cried again.

'Go away,' she sobbed; 'go away. Forget me. I have nothing to live for.' And just as Siegfried reached her and stretched out his arms to grasp her, she threw herself over the cliff edge. Horrified, he saw her fall like a stone; the waves closed over her head.

Prince Siegfried gathered up all his courage. 'I *must* save her,' he thought, 'even if I die in the attempt.' Without a moment's delay he leaped after her. The water was icy, and he came to the surface gasping for breath. There was no time to lose. He started to swim round and round, searching for her. But the seconds passed like hours, and he had almost given up hope of finding her alive, when his arm touched something soft.

'Odette,' he cried, as he took hold of her and turned towards the shore; 'speak to me!' She hung motionless in his arms. He quickly began to tire as he tried to swim and support the helpless girl. At last, after feeling as though he had been swimming for a lifetime, he reached the shore. Crawling on all fours, he dragged her out of the water and then collapsed exhausted.

For a long time he lay there as if he were dead. Then his strength began to come back to him, and at once he thought of Odette. Was she lying lifeless beside him? Had his struggle been

Prince Siegfried rescues Odette

in vain? He rolled over on his side and opened his eyes to look at her. His eyes opened wider and wider, and for a moment he thought he must be dreaming: Odette and all her friends were standing there, smiling at him.

'Oh Siegfried,' she said as she threw her arms around him, 'you've broken the spell!'

'Broken the spell?' echoed the Prince as he struggled to his feet.

'Yes,' she cried. 'You proved that you truly loved me when

you were ready to give your life to save me. Look! It's day-light already, and we have not changed to swans.'

Siegfried was too happy to speak. He forgot all his tiredness as he took Odette by the hand. Together they left the lakeside, followed by a throng of happy maidens and children. After pausing for a moment to look at a large owl, with closed eyes and ruffled feathers, lying dead in the grass, they walked quickly through the woods towards the castle.

Very soon flags would be flying above the lofty towers. Bells would ring out from distant churches. The road that twisted and turned as it climbed the hillside to the castle gateway would be thronged with people. They would be coming to the castle, to the wedding of Prince Siegfried and Odette.

CHAPTER VI

THE MUSIC

THE story of Prince Siegfried and Odette is known all over the world today, for, like the story of Prince Nutcracker, it was used for a ballet with music by Tchaikovsky. It too started as an old German tale.

You may see the title in French as 'Le Lac des Cygnes', which means The Lake of Swans, or Swans' Lake. The French word 'cygne' means 'swan' and is very much like our word for 'young swan'—'cygnet'. Ballets from many different countries often have their titles in French because for a long time France was the home of the ballet and ballet dancing.

The 'Swan Lake' ballet is really older than that of the 'Nut-cracker'. 'Swan Lake' was first performed in the Russian capital, St. Petersburg, in 1877, but the audience did not like it, and it was regarded as a failure. In 1890 'The Sleeping Beauty' ballet, with music by Tchaikovsky, was first given in St. Petersburg and, as you have already read, in 1892 the 'Nutcracker' ballet appeared. These were so successful that it was decided to produce 'Swan Lake' again, with some alterations. It appeared in 1895, and on this occasion it was so successful that it has appeared regularly ever since. If you live near a city you may be able to see it. If not, you may still enjoy the tunes, for Tchaikovsky's ballet music is so beautiful that it is often played and you can hear it at concerts or on the radio or the gramophone. Several of his pieces from 'Swan Lake' are very popular. There is the famous Waltz which begins with this tune on the violins:

The country people danced this waltz when they were invited to the castle to Prince Siegfried's twenty-first birthday party.

Another well-known piece is often called 'The Flight of the Swans'. The oboe plays this tune as the swans fly over the castle and Prince Siegfried and Benno decide to hunt them

Do you remember the cygnets dancing by the side of the lake during the night when Prince Siegfried and his friends followed the flight of the swans? 'The Dance of the Cygnets' opens with 'pom-pom-pom-pom' from the bassoons and then oboes and muted trumpets are heard playing this tune

Perhaps you can play these on the piano or on your recorder or violin. Even if you do not play an instrument, there is no need to wait to hear the music of 'Swan Lake' at a concert or on the radio. Try to get a record for your gramophone.

THE SLEEPING BEAUTY
and
THE FIREBIRD

THE SLEEPING BEAUTY
and
THE FIREBIRD

Illustrated by
ALAN CLARK

First published 1964
Sixth impression 1980

CONTENTS

The Sleeping Beauty

CHAPTER I

AURORA'S CHRISTENING

THE four trumpeters raised their golden instruments to their lips and played a fanfare which echoed through the lofty royal ballroom. The gilded doors were opened by huge negro guards and two more guests entered the room.

Waiting to greet them was the Lord High Chamberlain, Cantalbutte, in his ceremonial dress of black and gold. In a loud voice he announced their names; then the newcomers joined the lords and ladies already assembled. The doors closed again as Cantalbutte put on his spectacles, peered at his scroll on which the names of all the guests were written, and added two more ticks. Again the trumpets sounded and the doors opened. Again Cantalbutte's voice was heard as more guests arrived and had their names ticked off. Soon the room was full of noble lords and ladies who had been summoned by the King to witness the christening of his infant daughter, Princess Aurora.

From the ceiling hundreds of lights, in their crystal chandeliers, twinkled down on the scarlet and gold uniforms of the men and the bejewelled silks and velvets of their ladies. Flowers of all scents and sizes entwined the marble columns. The golden cradle of the infant princess, with the ever-watchful royal nursemaids, stood on a platform at one end of the room. Through the noise of trumpets, the announcements of Cantalbutte and the gossip of the guests, the Princess Aurora slept peacefully. At the other end of the room, on a higher platform and under crimson canopies, stood the empty thrones waiting for the King and Queen.

Suddenly the trumpets were heard again. This time they played louder and longer than before. The lords and ladies ceased their chatter and looked towards the doors. Putting his spectacles away, Cantalbutte stood to attention. The doors opened and King Florestan XXIV entered with his Queen, followed by a long train of attendants. The guests bowed as the Royal procession made its way slowly towards the cradle.

'How beautiful she is!' said the Queen, looking down on her golden-haired Aurora.

'A very good-natured and contented child!' replied the King. He took the Queen's arm and led her towards the thrones at the other end of the ballroom.

It was then the turn of the guests to file past and look into the cradle.

'She's just like an angel,' said one.

'Hair like pure gold,' remarked another.

'Look! she smiles in her sleep,' a third whispered, while a fourth was heard to say, 'How like her mother she is.'

Princess Aurora slept on and neither saw nor heard the guests as they passed by. When they had all seen the Princess, Cantalbutte's voice was heard again, announcing the arrival of the six fairy-godmothers. A fanfare greeted each fairy as she appeared. First came the Fairy of the Crystal Fountain, in a dress of sparkling whites and blues. She curtsied before the King and Queen, and then danced down the room towards the royal cradle. Near it she placed her gift, a crown of water-lilies. Wearing a floral dress, the Fairy of the Magic Garden came next, dancing her way to the cradle, gazing down on the sleeping infant, and putting her gift near the water-lily crown.

'The Fairy of the Woodland Glades!' shouted Cantalbutte as the next one entered, and she was soon followed by the Fairy of the Song Birds. The fifth Fairy, the Fairy of the Golden Vine, was in a dazzling dress of gold. She placed her gift alongside the others, the water-lily crown, the basket of flowers, the wild fruits of the woodlands, and the song-bird in the cage. The final fanfare rang out and everyone knew, from the colour of her

The Lilac Fairy

dress that it was the Lilac Fairy. After her curtsey she raised her wand as she smiled on the child. She was just going to place her gift with the others when a vivid flash of lightning made everyone jump. Before they recovered from their surprise, a terrific crack of thunder rocked the room. Princess Aurora awoke and cried.

CHAPTER II

THE CURSE OF CARABOSSE

BEFORE the sound of thunder had died away the ballroom doors burst open and a breathless messenger hurried towards Cantalbutte.

'Oh, sire,' he gasped as he fell on his knees before the Lord High Chamberlain, 'The Fairy Carabosse is approaching in her carriage.'

'The Fairy Carabosse,' echoed Cantalbutte, turning pale.

'Yes, sire,' continued the messenger. 'She is in a violent temper because you did not invite her to the christening. She is making the earth tremble with her thunder and splitting the skies with her lightning.'

'What is it, what is it?' shouted King Florestan from his throne. Cantalbutte, trembling all over, turned towards the King and Queen.

'Your Majesties,' he stammered, 'the Fairy Carabosse caused the lightning to flash and the thunder to peal. She is coming here now in a great temper.'

'Why, what has upset her?' the Queen asked.

'Oh, pardon me, your Majesties, but I forgot to invite her to the christening,' answered poor Cantalbutte, sinking still farther to the floor.

'You forgot!' roared the King, seizing the scroll from his

Lord High Chamberlain and looking quickly at the names of all the guests. 'You stupid nincompoop!' he screamed, throwing the scroll at Cantalbutte. His face became redder and redder, while the Queen went whiter and whiter. The poor Lord High Chamberlain shook in every limb and his teeth chattered in his nodding head.

With a sudden roar the doors flew open again. In rushed a coach pulled by four giant rats. Vultures flew overhead. As the coach jerked to a halt before the royal thrones a figure with gleaming green eyes, pointed nose, and long finger-nails alighted and strode up to the King. It was the wicked Fairy Carabosse. She was dressed in black from head to foot and carried a crooked stick in one hand.

'I demand an explanation!' she snarled. 'Why wasn't I invited to the christening?'

'It was all my fault,' said the unfortunate Cantalbutte. 'I assure you I did not mean to forget you. Please accept my humble apology.'

'Your fault,' said the fairy, turning to Cantalbutte. 'Take that! and that!' and she pulled him round the room by his hair and hit him with her stick.

'Mercy!' wailed the wretched Lord High Chamberlain, who was bruised all over and was losing great tufts of hair.

The Queen stepped down from her throne and pleaded with the angry fairy. 'Oh, Carabosse,' she said, 'do not spoil the christening. Please forgive us for forgetting to invite you, and be our guest for the day.'

'I'm not staying where I am not wanted,' replied Carabosse. 'I'm going, but before I go——'

'Mercy!' wailed the Lord High Chamberlain

'Yes?' said the Queen.

There was an evil glint in the fairy's eyes and a wicked grin on her face as she continued: 'Before I go I must not forget my gift to your infant child.' She looked round the room at all the anxious faces. 'My gift is a curse!' she screamed. There was a gasp of horror from the guests. 'The child will grow up to be beautiful. She will be strong and healthy, good and clever, but——' The wicked fairy paused and there was a deathly silence in the room. 'Before she is eighteen years old she will prick her finger and die.'

King Florestan's crown clattered to the floor. The sobbing Queen collapsed on her throne. With an unearthly cackle Carabosse jumped into her coach, cracked her whip and drove from the room. Outside, the lightning tore the skies and thunder rolled round the heavens. Inside, there was sadness and confusion. The king tried to console his heartbroken Queen. Cantalbutte wished he was dead. The tears of the nursemaids fell into the royal cradle. Suddenly the voice of the Lilac Fairy was heard.

'Pray do not grieve, your Majesties,' she said, 'for I have not yet made my gift to my god-child.'

Everyone turned to listen to the fairy in the lilac dress. The ladies dried their tears and even Cantalbutte looked more hopeful.

'My gift to the Princess Aurora,' the Lilac Fairy continued, 'is life, not death. One day she will prick her finger as the evil Fairy Carabosse said, but she will not die. She will fall into a long, deep sleep. She will sleep until a prince awakens her with a kiss.'

On hearing this good news the Lord High Chamberlain jumped in the air and danced a jig around the room. Full of joy, the King and Queen with the fairy-godmothers and all the guests gathered round the royal cradle. Princess Aurora was sleeping peacefully again.

CHAPTER III

AURORA'S BIRTHDAY

GRADUALLY the years passed by. King Florestan became a little fatter, the Queen's hair began to show touches of silver, and the Lord High Chamberlain got balder and balder. Princess Aurora, however, grew more beautiful each year, and everything possible was done to prevent her from pricking herself. Neither pins nor needles were allowed in the palace. Wherever the Princess went the royal nurse went too, always guarding her closely. They shielded her from prickly plants and long-clawed cats. All visitors to the palace were searched to see that they brought nothing with them that was sharp or pointed.

On Aurora's sixteenth birthday the palace grounds were crowded with people, for everyone in the country had been invited to her party. Lords and Ladies mingled with villagers in admiring the flowers, the fountains, and the strutting peacocks. Children chased each other over the lawns and counted the darting goldfish in the ponds. A great cheer rang out when the King and Queen with their attendants came down the path from the palace to the thrones set up by the edge of a large lawn on which the festivities were to take place. With them were four princes, an Indian prince, an Italian, a Polish, and an English prince, each of whom wished to marry Aurora. Hundreds of guests lined the edges of the lawn to watch the performance. First came a dance by village maidens who moved gracefully over the grass, each holding above her head a large hoop garlanded with flowers. Next it was Aurora's turn to entertain. There were gasps of admiration when the tall and graceful Princess, smiling with happiness, stepped forward to begin her dance. Her long silk dress, pale pink in colour, was studded with diamonds which flashed with her every movement. 'Encore!' the excited crowd shouted as her dance ended, and so the delighted Princess danced for them again. Afterwards, the four foreign princes were introduced to Aurora. Each of them danced with her in turn and presented her with a rose. This also pleased the on-lookers and so the four princes and Aurora came back and danced together.

Later, Aurora mingled with her guests around the lawn and watched the rest of the entertainment. She was enjoying a dance by the maids of honour when suddenly she felt someone touch her arm. On looking round she saw an old woman dressed from head to foot in black. Her back was bent, she was leaning on a crooked stick and her face was hidden behind a long black scarf. In one hand she held a strange object.

'This is a birthday gift for you, my dear,' she said, holding out a strange looking piece of wood to the Princess. Aurora was fascinated by this gift, for she had never seen anything like it before. She did not know that it was a spindle used in the spin-ning of wool from sheep. Almost every house in the country had its spinning wheel and spindle, but none could be found in the palace, for spindles were sharp and pointed, and spindles could prick.

'Thank you very much indeed,' said the Princess, but when she looked up the strange figure in black had disappeared. Aurora ran across the grass towards the royal thrones, carrying the spindle in one hand.

The birthday present

'What is that you have?' said the Queen anxiously, 'give it to me at once.'

'Oh, no mother, please, I want to keep it,' replied the Princess hiding it behind her back.

'Drop it this moment!' cried the Queen, rising to her feet. Full of mischief Aurora shook her head and danced away across the lawn, throwing the spindle from one hand to the other.

Poor Cantalbutte was again trembling from head to foot, for he knew that he would be blamed for the presence of the mysterious old woman in black. He had stood for hours by the gate making sure that nobody brought any scratchy object with them. He

She fell at their feet

had turned away four village women who were bringing their knitting and their knitting needles. Now he was watching the princess dance around holding a sharp spindle. It was all most distressing.

Suddenly Aurora stopped. She felt a twinge of pain shoot up her arm. She had pricked herself. Throwing away the spindle and sucking her blood-stained finger she hurried back towards her mother.

'Aurora! Aurora! What has happened?' said King Florestan anxiously as he hurried towards her with the Queen.

'Oh, it's nothing,' replied Aurora bravely, but she already had a strange feeling in her legs, and all the people seemed to her to be spinning round and round. She felt the grass coming up to meet her. She thought she saw an old woman in black laughing at her. She struggled on towards her mother and father and fell in a heap at their feet.

CHAPTER IV

THE ENCHANTMENT

THE birthday party which had begun so happily was now a scene of sadness and confusion. Hundreds of guests crowded round the spot where the Princess had fallen.

'Stand back, stand back, please!' urged the Lord High Chamberlain, but he pleaded in vain, for everyone wished to see what was happening. The Queen gently placed her arms around her daughter's shoulders and tried to raise her from the ground.

'Aurora!' she whispered, 'please speak to me, oh! speak to me.' But the Princess's body hung limply, as if she were dead. Her face was deathly white and the silvery pink dress was stained with blood from her finger. King Florestan, looking up from his daughter for a minute, saw a figure in black watching from behind a distant tree. The black scarf had fallen away from her, and he could recognize the evil face of the Fairy Carabosse.

'Seize that woman!' he commanded, and instantly the four foreign princes drew their swords and dashed after the wicked fairy who disappeared into the woods. At that moment the Lilac Fairy appeared as if from nowhere.

'Do not despair, your Majesties,' she said. 'Your daughter is not dead, she only sleeps. Carry her to her room and put her to bed.'

Before this could be done the sound of approaching footsteps made everyone turn. The four princes were coming back from the woods and it was plain to see that they had been unsuccessful. The Prince of England spoke for all of them.

The Sleeping Beauty

'I am sorry, your Majesty,' he said, bowing low, 'but the evil creature has escaped. We chased her here and there through the trees. Gradually we were getting nearer to her. She was almost within our grasp when there was a blinding flash and a cloud of smoke. When the smoke cleared she had vanished.'

'Thank you, all of you,' the King replied quietly. 'And now pray, carry my daughter into the palace.'

The four princes carefully lifted the sleeping girl and headed the procession along the winding paths, up the marble steps and

The palace is enchanted

through the wide doors into the palace. Across the great hall they went and up the red-carpeted staircase to Aurora's bedroom. They gently laid the princess on the bed and drew the bedclothes over her. Everyone stood back a little, leaving the King and Queen at the bedside looking down on their daughter. Even in deep sleep she was still beautiful, with her long, golden hair covering the pillows.

The Lilac Fairy raised her wand. Immediately everyone in the palace went to sleep just where they were. With closed eyes the King and Queen stood asleep at the bedside. The four foreign princes stood like statues. Nearby was Cantalbutte, perfectly still and no longer trembling. By the doors the Negro guards were motionless, like huge figures carved in ebony. Below in the courtyard the royal hounds, no longer watchful, squatted with closed eyes outside their kennels. The cook slept in her rocking chair, still holding a basin in one hand and clutching a spoon in the other. Only the Lilac Fairy was awake. Once more she raised her wand. In a twinkling, tall trees shot up through the lawns and flower-beds and completely surrounded the palace. Ivy and other creeping plants quickly climbed the walls and smothered the windows. Doorways disappeared behind a tangled growth of tall grasses. Thorny brambles crept and crawled like snakes over all the paths.

No longer could the palace be seen. No longer could the palace be reached and entered. The Lilac Fairy looked down on her work, smiled, and disappeared.

PRINCE CHARMING MEETS THE LILAC FAIRY

ONE hundred years passed and people forgot all about the sleeping Princess. The palace, completely buried by tall trees and tangled undergrowth, was also forgotten.

Our story now takes us to a far-off country, in which dwelt a young prince. His real name was Florimund, but, because of his handsome appearance most people called him Prince Charming. One morning he set off from his castle, accompanied by many noble Lords and Ladies, to hunt the wild boar. All day they searched without success for signs of these savage creatures, and, as evening came, they found themselves in a forest clearing by the side of a stream. There they sat down to eat and rest while the servants opened the baskets of food and wine.

'Come on!' said one of the ladies, after they had finished the meal, 'let us have games and dances. This clearing is just the place for them.'

Quickly a target was set up and shooting practice began. Arrows whizzed through the air and a great cheer rang out whenever someone scored a bull's-eye. When they tired of shooting they played other games and when they tired of games they turned to dancing. Everyone was happy except the Prince. He joined in neither the games nor the dancing, but sat some distance away on a fallen tree-trunk, with his head in his hands. He was tired of life at the castle, with its endless round of games and dancing, of feasting and hunting. How he wished that he could go on a real adventure. He imagined himself riding off with shield and spear to kill a dangerous dragon, or saving a beautiful maiden from the clutches of an evil witch. He was tired of having nothing to do but enjoy himself.

Suddenly, a wild boar was sighted some distance away. The dancing stopped, spears were seized, and everybody dashed off in pursuit. Only the Prince remained, still sitting there as darkness came and the moon cast its reflection on the water. For a while everything was silent. Then the Prince heard a movement from the stream. He looked towards it and saw a boat coming in his direction. It was not an ordinary boat, for its sides were made of mother-of-pearl, and from its prow silken threads rose into the air where they were harnessed to giant butterflies which pulled the vessel along. Slowly it glided to the water's edge and someone stepped out. It was the Lilac Fairy.

'Good day, Prince Charming,' she greeted him, 'why do you sit alone in the forest at nightfall? Where are your companions?'

'Oh, they are hunting the wild boar,' he replied. 'They are always hunting wild boar, or playing games like small children, or making themselves dizzy with dancing.'

'Well, what would you rather do?' the Fairy asked.

'Something quite different,' answered the Prince, 'something exciting and worth-while, something I have never done before.'

The Lilac Fairy was silent for a while. Then she said, 'How would you like to go to a distant land and find the Sleeping Beauty?'

'The Sleeping Beauty?' said the astonished Prince. 'I have never heard of her. Who is she?'

Sitting down beside him the Lilac Fairy told the story of the lovely Aurora, the evil Carabosse, and the forgotten palace.

Prince Charming meets the Lilac Fairy

'A pretty tale,' said the Prince, when she had finished, 'but it is not true, is it?'

'Quite true,' replied the Lilac Fairy. 'Look, I will show you the Sleeping Beauty.'

She waved her wand and in the clouds appeared a picture of

Aurora in her bed surrounded by all the sleeping figures. She raised her wand again, the picture vanished and another came. Aurora was dancing on the grass at her sixteenth birthday party.

'How beautiful she is,' sighed the Prince. 'Please tell me how I can find her.'

'Come along,' said the Lilac Fairy. 'I will take you.'

Together they boarded the boat which glided away downstream. No sound was heard save for the lapping of the waves and the beating wings of the butterflies. They sailed for hundreds of miles through many countries. They sailed through autumn, where brown and gold leaves dropped on the water. They sailed through winter, with its ice and snow. Soon it was spring. The birds sang and the trees were covered with blossom. The sun shone more strongly still and they sailed into summer.

'We are nearly there,' said the Lilac Fairy.

CHAPTER VI

THE SPELL IS BROKEN

LOWLY the boat came to rest at the stream's edge and Prince Charming helped the Lilac Fairy to alight. Before them stood a dense wood. The Lilac Fairy seemed to know the Prince's thoughts, for she suddenly said:

'Yes, this is the wood which hides the palace. We are its first visitors for one hundred years.'

The Prince stood looking at the tall trees rising everywhere

Before them stood a dense wood

* 23 *

from the tangled mass of creeping plants. He glanced up at the spreading branches which shut out the daylight, then turning to the Fairy he said:

'Surely we need an army of woodcutters to hack a path through this wood to the palace!'

The secret path

'Oh, no!' she replied, 'there is a path known only to me. Follow and I will show you.' She led him round the edge of the wood until they came to a weeping-willow tree. Parting its drooping branches with her wand, she beckoned the Prince to enter. They found themselves in a low tunnel, with branches just above their heads and the trunks of trees rising on either side. Carefully they made their way over gnarled roots and crackling twigs in almost complete darkness. Startled rabbits scurried away as they approached. Blind-flying bats brushed against their faces. The path twisted this way and that as it went, but the Lilac Fairy knew the way and the Prince followed close behind her. He was wondering how much farther they had to go when the fairy stopped and pointed towards the ground. In the gloom, the Prince could just see a flight of stone steps leading upwards. A carpet of moss covered each step and pointed ferns peeped through the cracks in the stonework. The two figures climbed slowly upwards until they found themselves in the courtyard of the palace. They stepped over the sleeping hounds and reached an ivy-covered door. Startled birds flew from their shelter as the Lilac Fairy and Prince Charming tore down long streamers of ivy, opened the door, and walked along a corridor curtained with cobwebs. They passed the kitchens where the cook still slept in her rocking-chair, with tarnished spoon in one hand, the dust-filled bowl in the other. They came to the great hall, now damp and gloomy, for no light passed through its tree-covered windows. Up the main staircase they felt their way, past silent footmen and sleeping maidservants, until they reached the door of Aurora's bedroom. The negro guards were no longer guarding. Motionless they stood as the Prince and the Lilac Fairy passed them and entered the bed-room.

The Prince could not help giving a gasp of surprise at the sight before him. There on the bed was the sleeping princess. On one side stood King Florestan and his Queen, with the Lord High Chamberlain, Cantalbutte, behind them. On the other side stood the foreign princes with their attendants.

'Have these people been standing up asleep for a hundred years?' the startled Prince exclaimed.

'For one hundred years exactly,' replied the Lilac Fairy.

The Prince moved on tiptoe to the edge of the bed as if he was afraid that a noise would awaken the sleepers. He looked on the face of Aurora with her golden hair still gleaming on the pillow.

'How beautiful she is,' he whispered as he leaned over and kissed her cold lips. He moved away quickly, held his breath, and waited to see what would happen. Slowly the Princess turned on to her back, opened her eyes and smiled at the Prince. At the same time there were other movements in the room. The King and Queen came towards the bed as if they had never been asleep at all, and old Cantalbutte trotted behind them. The four foreign princes opened their eyes and continued a conversation they had been having one hundred years earlier. The room suddenly became bright when the Lilac Fairy waved her wand and the wood outside disappeared. Sunlight streamed in and the dust and cobwebs vanished. Outside, the lawns and flower beds, the lakes and the fountains could be seen again, just as they had been a century before, on Aurora's sixteenth birthday. The silence of the palace was broken, and everywhere there was happy and excited chatter.

'Oh, my Aurora!' sighed the Queen, as she held her daughter close to her. Tears of joy were running down her face.

'How can I thank you?' said the King, as he grasped the Prince's hand. Before the Prince could reply, King Florestan continued: 'Oh—I know, I suppose you wish to marry my daughter?'

'If your Majesty pleases,' murmured the Prince, bowing low.

'Certainly, my boy, certainly!' And the excited King gave the Prince a hearty pat on his back and dashed off to join the Queen. The Lord High Chamberlain, who had overheard the conversation rubbed his hands with delight, for there was nothing he liked better than organizing christenings, birthdays, and weddings. Prince Charming, left on his own, went over to join Aurora.

'Come along,' she said to him, 'let me show you our beautiful gardens.' He took her hand and together they made their way out into the sunshine.

CHAPTER VII

AURORA'S WEDDING

THE royal ballroom in King Florestan's palace was once more filled with guests. This time they had come, not to a christening, nor to a birthday party, but to the wedding of Prince Charming and Princess Aurora. From the ceiling the hundreds of lights, in their crystal chandeliers, again twinkled down on scarlet and gold uniforms and bejewelled silks and velvets. The King and Queen sat enthroned under the crimson canopies. The Lord High Chamberlain, Cantalbutte, determined that nothing should go wrong this time, rushed hither and thither seeing that all orders were being obeyed. Then, like a faithful sheepdog, he returned to his place at the King's side.

Suddenly, the four trumpeters raised their golden instruments and played a fanfare. The doors opened, and the bride and bridegroom entered, followed by their bridesmaids and pages and also by the six fairy-godmothers. How lovely Aurora looked as she walked arm in arm with her beloved husband, smiling and acknowledging the bowing and curtsying of her guests.

Again the trumpets rang out and again the doors opened. There was a murmur of excitement in the room as a strange procession entered. The people of storyland were coming to offer their gifts and to dance at the wedding.

* 28 *

'Look!' said one of the guests, 'there's Puss in Boots with the white cat.'

'Yes, and do you see who's coming in now? It's little Red Riding Hood with the wolf close behind her.'

The giant and Hop o' my Thumb

'Why, there's Cinderella and her Prince!' another guest exclaimed, 'but I don't know the golden-haired girl talking to them.'

'Don't you?' someone answered. 'Why, that's Goldilocks.' There was a gasp of surprise as a huge giant entered, stooping as he did so, in order to get through the door. Clinging tightly to his shoulder was Hop o' my Thumb, and not far behind came Beauty and the Beast. The guests moved back towards the walls, leaving a space in the centre of the ballroom, where these well-beloved characters from Fairy Tale and Nursery Rhyme could dance in honour of the bride and bridegroom.

Everyone enjoyed the dance of Puss-in-Boots and the White Cat, and there was great excitement when poor little Red Riding Hood, with her basket of food was chased and caught

Off on their honeymoon

by the wicked wolf. Everyone laughed at the antics of the tiny Hop o' my Thumb and the giant, and admired the graceful movements of Cinderella and her Prince. There was much clapping and cheering when the performance ended, and the cheering broke out again when it became known that Prince Charming and Aurora were going to dance also.

So the happy party went on, with neither thunder and lightning nor wicked fairies to spoil it. The Fairy Carabosse was forgotten. She had not been seen for many years, and some said that she had been killed by one of her own flashes of lightning. Before the party ended the King and Queen, Prince Charming and Princess Aurora, and all the guests joined in the dancing, and the room was filled with graceful movement.

Soon it was time for the Prince and Princess to depart for their honeymoon. The guests followed them from the palace, down the paths and past the flower beds to the banks of the stream. Raising her wand, the Lilac Fairy blessed the happy pair. The mother-of-pearl boat glided to the bank and the Prince and Princess entered. The wings of the butterflies began to beat, slowly at first and then faster. The boat moved away amid cries of 'Good-bye' and the waving of hands. The King and Queen stood there with their guests until they could no longer see their daughter and the boat was a mere speck in the distance.

CHAPTER VIII

THE MUSIC

ABOUT three hundred years ago a Frenchman named Charles Perrault was writing fairy tales. Perrault was born in the year 1628, and before his death in 1703 his story-writing had made him famous. Although you may never have heard of him by name, you are sure to know some of his stories. They include 'Little Red Riding Hood', 'Puss in Boots', 'Cinderella', 'Tom Thumb', and 'The Sleeping Beauty'. He wrote them in French, of course, and the French title for 'The Sleeping Beauty' is '*La Belle au Bois Dormant*', which really means 'The Beauty in the Sleeping Wood'.

Today these fairy tales are known all over the world. Small children love to listen as they are told to them. Later they read them for themselves. When they are still older they meet them once again at the theatre, for many of Perrault's tales have been used in pantomime and ballet.

You have most probably been to a pantomime at Christmas. Quite often a pantomime has a fairy-tale title such as *Cinderella*, but the entertainment includes much more than the well-known story. In between scenes from the fairy tales there are the singers of comic songs, the clowns, the acrobats, the jugglers, and the dancers, all of whom have really nothing whatever to do with the fairy tale. Today a pantomime is more like a variety show and not at all like ballet, which tells the story through movement and dancing to the music of an orchestra, without using any words at all. Strangely enough, pantomime used to be quite like ballet a long time ago, for the word 'pantomime' means the telling of a story by miming, that is, without speech.

The story of the Sleeping Beauty that you have just read is the first half of Perrault's tale, which has been used for many years both in pantomime and ballet. At one time the title of the ballet was changed to *The Sleeping Princess* so that people would not mistake it for the pantomime. Today, however, the ballet is once more called *The Sleeping Beauty*.

The music for *The Sleeping Beauty* was written by Tchaikovsky. This famous Russian composer had already written the music for another well-known ballet, *Swan Lake*. In the year 1890, in the Russian capital of St. Petersburg, now Leningrad, *The Sleeping Beauty* was performed for the first time. Not long afterwards, Tchaikovsky started to write the music for the ballet *Nutcracker*. Today these three ballets with music by Tchaikovsky—*Swan Lake*, *The Sleeping Beauty*, and *Nutcracker*—are regularly performed in towns and cities throughout the world. You may be fortunate enough to see a performance. If not, you can still enjoy the music when it is performed on the radio or television, or can listen to some of it on gramophone records. Perhaps you play an instrument yourself. If so, try these tunes from The Sleeping Beauty on the piano, violin, recorder, or whatever instrument you play.

THE MUSIC

1. There are many famous waltzes in Tchaikovsky's ballet music. Do you remember the 'Waltz of the Flowers' in the *Nutcracker* ballet? Here is part of the well-known waltz from Act One of *The Sleeping Beauty*. It is the dance of the village maidens at Aurora's sixteenth birthday party.

2. This melody also comes in Act One during Aurora's sixteenth birthday party. It is known as the 'Rose Adagio'. You will remember that in the story the four foreign princes dance with Aurora and each presents her with a rose.

3. This is the Lilac Fairy's tune and occurs several times. It is heard when the Lilac Fairy orders that the sleeping Princess should be carried into the palace. It is heard again when the

Lilac Fairy, in the mother-of-pearl boat, meets Prince Charming as he sits alone in the forest clearing.

4. This melody is heard when Prince Charming steps into the Lilac Fairy's boat to go with her to discover the sleeping Princess.

5. This is heard in Act Three at the wedding celebrations when the people from fairyland give their performance. It is the beginning of the dance of Little Red Riding Hood and the Wolf. If you see a performance or hear a recording, look out for this tune on the woodwind, followed later by the growling of the wolf (strings).

6. This is also taken from the wedding celebrations in Act Three. The fairy-tale characters have finished their performance, and this is the beginning of Aurora's dance.

The Firebird

CHAPTER I

PRINCE IVAN GOES HUNTING

THROUGHOUT the day the sun had shone down on the village from a cloudless sky. It was the hottest day of the summer. Huge cracks were appearing in the parched earth, and the river, which had roared under the bridge all winter, was now a mere trickle. The green carpet of the fields had faded to one of yellows and browns. The small cottages were almost as hot as ovens, and everywhere people could be seen squatting out of doors in the shadows of their houses. Children sat outside too, wondering how to pass the time, for it was too hot to run and play. Mothers sang quietly as they nursed their fretful babies. Dogs crouched panting, their long tongues lolling from open jaws.

It was just as hot in the palace on the hill. It made the King angry, and he was forever shouting to his perspiring attendants, urging them to fan him more vigorously. The water in the marble ponds of the palace gardens was no longer cool, and the goldfish hid themselves under the huge floating lily-leaves. Beneath the palm trees in the courtyard Prince Ivan sat and talked to his friends for it was too hot to go hunting. Everyone, from the King down to the poorest peasant, rested and waited for the golden red ball of the sun to sink behind the western mountains.

With the evening came a refreshing breeze, and the village sprang to life. People began their neglected work, children played games, and the dogs sniffed about for food. The tired babies closed their eyes and fell asleep. The Prince Ivan decided to go for a long walk. Picking up his bow and arrows he opened the small gate in the palace wall and strode off in the direction of the forest. Soon he was walking silently and with a spring in each step on the carpet of leaf mould and pine needles in the gloom of the tall trees. From time to time he took quick aim at ghostly-looking owls and blind-flying bats, but in the dusk he missed his mark and lost his arrows.

After following the winding paths for several miles Ivan

decided to retrace his steps. Before long, however, he realized that he was lost, for night had fallen and the paths were no longer to be seen. He crashed helplessly through the under-growth and stumbled over the roots of trees. Suddenly he saw

Lost in the forest

something tall and greyish-white in front of him. He cautiously approached it and found it was a high wall that he had never seen before in all his forest wanderings. It was useless to try to climb it in the darkness, so he sat down with his back against it, deciding to rest there until daybreak. All was still and silent and dark, and very soon the Prince was fast asleep.

CHAPTER II

THE FIREBIRD

IVAN awoke with a start. He wondered what had disturbed him, for it was still night, and he could neither see nor hear anything in the darkness around him. He stared into the gloom and listened, but he was still very sleepy and before long his eyes were closing and his head nodding. Suddenly he was wide awake again as a bright light lit up the near-by trees and cast long dark shadows on the ground. This light, which danced about and made the shadows dance with it, seemed to be coming from over the high wall against which the Prince had been resting.

His eyes were closing and his head nodding

* 40 *

After a few minutes it vanished as quickly as it had come, and night returned to the forest.

'Most mysterious,' said Ivan to himself. 'If this strange light comes again I must find out what it is.'

He had not long to wait before it reappeared. Quickly his fingers and toes searched for cracks in the wall as he pulled himself up. When he reached the top and looked over, his eyes opened wide with amazement. Below him was a long green lawn surrounded by flowering shrubs and apple trees. The trees were laden with fruit, not ordinary fruit, but golden fruit which glittered in the light. Gliding in and out of the trees was a magnificent bird. Its long yellow and red feathers glowed like fire. Its eyes flashed like diamonds. Its wings were like flames. The curious light which had awakened the Prince was coming from this brilliant bird, and went with it as it flew backwards and forwards. Ivan's hands moved unthinkingly to his cross-bow, but he quickly drew them away.

'No, no!' he murmured to himself, 'I must not kill it, I will try to catch it and take it back with me to the palace. I have never seen a bird so beautiful. It is no ordinary bird, it is a bird of fire.'

Silently he climbed down into the garden and crept between the bushes towards the Firebird which was pecking at the golden apples on one of the trees. Nearer and nearer he crawled, and still the bird did not see him as it fluttered from one fruit to another. Ivan made a sudden dart forward and the bird was struggling in his hands. In vain it tried to escape. Its dazzling wings beat against his face and its shining beak pecked at his hands, but he refused to let it go. At last, tired with struggling,

The Firebird escapes

the Firebird sank exhausted in the Prince's arms. He almost dropped it with surprise when he heard it speaking to him.

'Let me go, please let me go', it whimpered. Ivan found himself speaking back to it.

'No, no!' he said, 'I will not harm you, but I am taking you with me back to the palace.' The bird, in a last effort to save itself, turned its head and plucked a long orange-coloured feather from one of its wings.

'Take this,' it said, offering the feather to the Prince. 'Whenever you are in danger, wave this feather and I will come to your aid.' As Ivan lifted one hand and took the feather, the Firebird slipped from his grasp and flew away over the trees. Away it flew, getting smaller and smaller, until it finally disappeared and all was dark again.

CHAPTER III

A BALL GAME

IVAN sat under one of the trees laden with golden apples and waited for the night to end. Never before in all his visits to the forest had he seen this garden. At the palace of his father, the King, he had never heard anyone mention such a place and so he was determined to explore its every corner in the light of day before setting out on his homeward journey. He was too excited to sleep any more so he sat with his back against the tree-trunk and waited for the dawn. He had not long to wait, for daybreak comes early in the summer time. Soon the sky changed from black to grey and forest birds greeted the morning with their songs. Before long the clouds were tinged with gold when the first rays of the sun appeared. Ivan could now see clearly everything around him. He got up, rubbed his eyes and yawned as he stretched himself.

He found that the high wall over which he had climbed completely enclosed the garden, but in one of its sides there was a huge door set in a stone archway. He ran quickly to it, curious to find out what lay beyond, but it was bolted and barred on the other side. He pushed against it and tried to shake it but it would not yield. Its stout oak panels were as strong as the wall itself. 'If I cannot go through the wall I must climb over it,' he said to himself. Just then he heard a noise on the other side so he darted behind a bush and waited.

Slowly the huge door creaked open and a group of barefooted maidens, in long white dresses, came running through on to the lawn. Ivan counted them. 'One, two, three . . . twelve altogether.' He had no sooner finished than another maiden appeared. She was the most beautiful girl he had ever seen. Her

Another maiden appeared

long golden hair floated behind her as she ran to join the others. 'She must be their leader,' thought Ivan, 'or perhaps she is a princess,' for although she was dressed in white like the others, her long gown was richly embroidered with thread of gold. The girls danced over the grass and up to the apple trees. They shook the branches and a shower of golden fruit fell to the ground. With shouts of joy they darted here and there picking them up. Ivan, from his leafy hiding place watched and wondered. 'Surely they cannot eat such fruit,' he thought, 'why do they gather it?'

He soon discovered the answer, for games began and the shining apples took the place of rubber balls. They flew through the air into hands outstretched to catch them. Back again they were hurled, gleaming and glittering as they went. There were shrieks when a player failed to make a catch. One apple, hitting the ground, rolled towards where the Prince was hidden. It came to rest almost at his feet. Picking it up he stepped from behind the bush and walked towards the maidens. A hush fell on the garden and the games ceased when the startled girls saw the stranger coming towards them. They crowded together behind the girl in the embroidered dress. Ivan went up to her and, bowing low, held out the apple. She hesitated for a while, as if afraid, and then she quickly took it.

'Thank you,' she said, 'but—you startled us, sir, suddenly appearing from nowhere.'

'Not from nowhere,' Ivan replied, 'but from behind that bush. Last night, when walking in the forest, I saw this wall and climbed over it. I spent the night here and hid when you approached. My name is Ivan. Pray tell me yours.'

'Oh, I am the Princess', she answered, 'but there is no time for us to talk. You must leave this garden at once, for you are in great danger.'

'Danger?' asked the Prince. 'Surely you girls will not attack me!'

'No, no,' said the Princess, 'but you are in the garden of the wizard Koschtchei*.'

'Koschtchei,' Ivan echoed, 'I have never heard of him, but I am prepared to do battle with him.'

'You cannot fight him with ordinary weapons,' said the Princess anxiously. 'He will cast a spell and make you his slave.'

'Or turn you to stone,' another girl added.

'Or torture you,' said another.

'Escape before it is too late,' pleaded the Princess, 'for we ourselves cannot escape: we are all under his spell and must remain here in his castle for ever. Only for one hour each day are we allowed out into this garden.'

'I will not go and leave you to this evil monster,' the Prince retorted, 'I have never yet run away from danger and will not do so now.'

Just then a great gong boomed out and the frightened girls fled quickly through the archway. Surprised by this sudden move, the Prince stood for a few moments and watched the retreating figures. Then he raced after them, but he was too late. The great gates closed in his face, and once again he was alone in the garden.

* Pronounced Kush-chay.

CHAPTER IV

IN KOSCHTCHEI'S POWER

KNOWING that he could not force open the gates Ivan started to climb the high wall, for he was determined to rescue the Princess and her friends from the wizard's power. His progress was slow and difficult, for the garden side of the wall was very smooth and footholds were few. So occupied was he with his task, and so quiet was the garden, that a sudden loud noise startled him and he almost fell to the ground. The gates burst open and masses of weird figures poured in, running, leaping, stumbling, and crawling. Once these had been ordinary men, but now they were Koschtchei's creatures, transformed by his spells into misshapen monsters. Some had huge heads with eyes as big as saucers and teeth like tigers'. Others had long arms which almost touched the ground as they ambled along like apes. A few, with outstretched hands, tried to feel their way forward for they were blind. All of them ran hither and thither, this way and that, like a pack of hounds seeking their prey.

At last they saw the Prince clinging to the wall and, screaming and screeching, they ran towards him. Long arms reached upwards and pulled him to the ground. Strong arms seized him and dragged him to the middle of the lawn. Then a sudden hush fell over the garden. The monsters drew back, leaving

Suddenly the gate burst open

Ivan standing alone, as other figures were seen approaching through the gateway. First came Koschtchei's bodyguard of twenty negroes with glistening black bodies and leopard-skin cloaks. Behind them was the evil wizard himself, a terrifying figure. Cruel eyes stared from his deathly white face, with its hook nose and pointed beard. His long thin legs and arms, his hunched back over which there was a black cloak, gave him the appearance of a huge beetle. Silently he approached the Prince and fixed his evil eyes on him. Slowly he raised his arms before him with his outstretched fingers pointing towards Ivan. He was about to put the Prince under a spell.

Suddenly his magic making was interrupted. The beautiful Princess and her twelve companions ran into the garden and up to where the wizard stood. On bended knees and with tears in their eyes they implored Koschtchei to spare the Prince. He snarled at them and bade his guards take them away. Turning towards Ivan he raised his hands again and muttered strange words. The Prince sank to the ground as he felt the strength leaving his body. He was powerless to defend himself. He wondered what evil Koschtchei was planning. Was he to be killed, or tortured, or changed into a horrible monster? For a second time the wizard raised his hands. Ivan

The evil wizard

could see Koschtchei's lips moving as he spoke, but he could no longer hear him. He felt a strange numbness in his limbs. The wizard's hands rose for a third time. It was then that Ivan remembered the feather that the Firebird had given him. Summoning his remaining strength he pulled it from his pocket and waved it weakly in the air.

CHAPTER V

THE MAGIC EGG

A<small>T</small> once Ivan's signal for help was answered. The Firebird suddenly appeared in a blaze of light. Swooping down from the sky, it dived swiftly towards Koschtchei. Its fiery feathers brushed against him as it passed, and the wizard staggered back bewildered. Down the bird came

The Firebird to the rescue

again, but this time it flew low over the heads of the wizard's monsters and his bodyguard, and their eyes were dazzled by its brilliance. It continued its low circling: there was magic in its movements. All who watched it were drawn towards it. They were attracted by its flaming colours as moths are to a light. They followed it as the children followed the Pied Piper. Across the grass and round the apple trees it glided with the monsters never far behind. At first they were trotting slowly after it, but soon the Firebird began to fly more quickly and the trotting changed to running. Faster still the Firebird flew, between the bushes, round the trees, across the lawn and back again, and still the evil monsters rushed after it. Even Koschtchei, whose magic was not as strong as the Firebird's, had been compelled to join the chase. Again the bird increased its speed, but it was too much for the pursuers. Panting and puffing, gasping and groaning, they sank down on the ground exhausted. The Firebird then flew over them with a slow swaying movement and soon the wizard and all his company were asleep.

'Now is your chance,' said the Firebird, alighting near the Prince. 'While Koschtchei and all his creatures sleep, go to his castle and seize the egg.'

'The egg?' asked the puzzled Prince.

'In Koschtchei's den,' said the bird, 'is a golden casket. In the casket is a large white egg as large as a man's head. Break the egg and Koschtchei with all his evil will disappear. Go quickly now!'

Jumping over the sleeping bodies, Ivan ran out through the archway, and up the stone stairway into the deserted castle. He went quickly from room to room, his footsteps echoing through the empty building. At last he found the wizard's den with its books and bottles, its snake skins and skulls. In a large cupboard he found what he was seeking. Carrying the shining casket in both hands he made his way back to the garden. The

Koschtchei pleaded for his life

sleeping figures were beginning to move, tossing and turning as they awakened. Going quickly to the centre of the lawn, where not long before he had suffered from Koschtchei's magic, Ivan put the casket on the ground and raised the lid. By this time everybody had woken up. They heard Koschtchei's cry of terror as the Prince lifted the giant egg and held it up for all to see. He tossed it high in the air, and the wizard screamed again, but Ivan caught it safely as it fell. Koschtchei, with every limb trembling, staggered up to the Prince and fell grovelling at his feet. While he pleaded for his life Ivan taunted him by tossing the egg lightly from one hand to the other. Finally, tired of teasing, Ivan dashed the egg to the ground. There was a deafening noise as it shattered into thousands of pieces and everything went dark for a while.

When the light returned Koschtchei and his castle had disappeared. No trace was left of the wizard and his evil. Monsters had become men again and the blind could see. How excited they all were when they realized the spell had been broken! Some sang and danced, others cried with joy. The Princess, followed by her friends, made her way through the happy crowd until she found the Prince.

'We wish to thank you,' she said as she curtsied low before him, 'for our freedom.'

'Do not thank me,' replied Ivan, 'you must thank the Firebird'—but that had disappeared too.

After the wedding

CHAPTER VI

PRINCE IVAN MARRIES

THE hot summer had ended and autumn had come, bringing with it some gentle rain. The earth was no longer parched and the faded fields were green again. Brown, russet, and yellow leaves decorated the trees and the village was decorated too. Flags and streamers hung from every window. Villagers in their best clothes thronged the streets. People had come from miles around to see the wedding of Prince Ivan and the Princess. They all rushed forward when the Prince arrived at the church in a golden carriage drawn by four white horses. They bowed and curtsied as the King and Queen drew near. They rushed forward again when the Princess appeared with her twelve maidens. The great church was crowded and hundreds who could not get in stood outside in groups, waiting until the service ended. At last the bells rang out from the tower and heralds played a fanfare on their trumpets. There was a great cheer when the bride and bridegroom came down the steps arm in arm. All eyes were on the happy pair, or nearly all eyes. Some who looked up said that they saw a large bird circling over the village, a bird with bright yellow and red feathers which glowed like a fire, a bird whose eyes flashed like diamonds, a bird with wings like flames.

CHAPTER VII

THE MUSIC

ABOUT how many words do you think there are in the Firebird story that you have just read? Make a guess before looking for the answer at the bottom of this page.*
I think that you will agree this is a large number, yet strangely enough, this story is often told without using any words at all. This is done by turning it into a ballet. In ballet there is no speaking as there is in a play—the story is told by miming and dancing. There are costumes and scenery and, because of the dancing, orchestral music is always an important part of ballet.

The music of *Firebird* was composed by Igor Stravinsky, who was born near the Russian city of St. Petersburg, now called Leningrad, in 1882. This ballet was first performed in Paris in 1910 and was a great success. Its French title is *L'Oiseau de Feu* (oiseau = bird, feu = fire). Later, Stravinsky arranged a suite from the ballet, known as the 'Firebird' suite, which is often performed at concerts. Try to see this ballet if you can. If not, perhaps you will be able to get a recording of the 'Firebird' suite for your record-player. You will need to play it more than once—in fact, many times, before you will really get to know it. There are not many tunes in this suite that you can successfully play on the piano, violin, or recorder, but here are three for you to try.

* About 3,200.

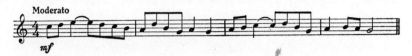

The tune above, and the one below are heard when Ivan meets the Princesses in the garden (Chapter III).

The tune above is taken from a Russian folk-song.

The next tune is heard when the story reaches its happy ending and Koschtchei and his castle have disappeared (Chapter V). This tune also is from a Russian folk-song.